ORTEGA COMICS LIFE IN LA

CALEB CARTER

Illustrations by Lisa Brennan
kitty.callie@yahoo.com

ABOUT THE AUTHOR

CALEB CARTER was born in New Orleans, Louisiana. At the age of seven he moved to South Central, Los Angeles with his family. Many of the Ortega's characters are inspired by actual friends of his.

proud of our children
Our son is in medical school and our daughter is in law school

And your other son is ... is ....

fitness expert. started curling welve ounce cans, but now I'm up to forty ounce bottles of beer!

Maybe he'll be a writer, Maria. Gotta admit that took some creativity.

Lookin good, chica!
Yeah, sexy mama, look like you outta be with me!
Hector, can you please keep those friends of yours under control when I'm home!
Sal, Sammy, Shonda's my sister. Show some respect. Be on your best behavior.
Good girls like bad guys
After ten years maybe you oughta move on
She's softening up
ha ha ha
ha ha ha
ha ha
ha ha
ha ha ha
ha ha
ha
ha
ha
ha
See, she's giddy with excitement
Or ridicule

Armando, can you please talk to your brother about making a serious career choice?
Sure Mom.
Mom wants me to--
I heard. And if my rap career don't work out I'm gonna be a politician.
Really? Weren't you accused of trespassing last month?
I was practicing Watergate.
What about your illegal cigarettes?
I puff but I don't inhale.
And that car you borrowed without permission?
I am not a crook!
Did you have that talk with your brother, Armando?
Yeah. Strange as it may sound that kid might actually run the country someday.

So this is your first day as a substitute teacher. Good luck, Hakeem.
Thanks, Shonda
SCHO
Mr. Hakeem, Hakeem is the name of a famous basketball player. Do you play basketball?
No
Do you sing, Mr. Hakeem?
No, I don't sing. I don't dance. I don't rap, and I don't play sports. I am a substitute teacher. I educate.
I understand. You gotta do something when you don't have any talent.

SURF PRO
If you're a surf pro how come I never see you in the water?

SURF PRO
My style is so flamboyant when I surf I need the whole beach.
You're no surf pro. This just a gimmick for a loser like you to meet girls.

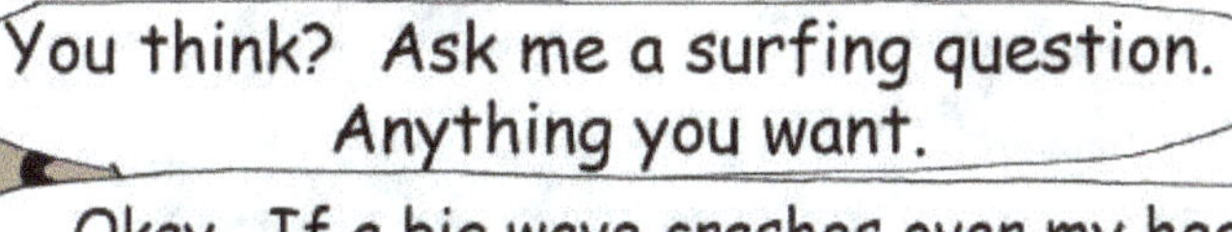

You think? Ask me a surfing question. Anything you want.
Okay. If a big wave crashes over my head and knocks me off my board, what should I do?
Swim for your life and try not to drown-clown!

SURF PRO
You call that advice? I knew you were fake!
That's the free version. For fifty bucks I throw in shark survival skills too.

RAP MASTER ..

Rock on Hector !
You the man

Dont step to me cause Im'a gangsta
If I dont like you Im'a shank ya

I wanna drink more beer !

Beer!
Beer!
Beer!
Beer!

Hector, doesn't it bother you that you personify a negative image of a Latino male?

You even gotta preach when I`m having a good dream don`t ya !

What?

Can I take your picture for my presentation at the Elementary School?
Sure

Hey, do you want our picture for your presentation too?
Sure. Say cheese and I'll snap it

Kids, be like these guys, college educated and law school students.   Don't be like the guys in my other hand. High School drop-outs with no jobs.

Did our picture help to inspire the kids?
Absolutely.

Here in LA police abuse and misconduct is embedded in the culture.
Body cams and dash cams have helped some but not enough.
We must fight to end qualified immunity! Tax payers shouldn't have to pay for their misdeeds.
I pulled you over because I saw an alien beam down from a spaceship and get into your car.
THAT'S FREAKING RIDICULOUS!!!
So sue me! Where's your papers?!

Shonda, if you had to make a choice between two handsome vato's like us, which one would you choose?
Yeah, which?

Well--
I know it's a tough choice. Either way you win, right?

If I had to make a choice, I would choose the one that would stop drinking, fighting, and smoking.

The one who would be willing to get a job and become a responsible member of society

Your sister Shonda is almost perfect, but she's got one major character flaw.
What's that? High expectations?

Keep it in the real world!
Naw, impossible standards, man!

"Three months later..."

Let me get this straight. We bet ten bucks on who can get a girl's number first, and twenty-five bucks on who can get a kiss first, right?
Right.
You're on.

Hector you beautiful man candy and great rapper. Call me, please!

Hey, you didn't even to talk to that girl. You set this up.
Did not. I've never met Lucy before.

Lucy! How'd you know her name if you never met her?
Uh...intuition? Yeah, that's it. Gimmie my money!

Shonda, Hakeem, wanna hear my new rap?
Not now, Hector. We're studying.
This one is the bomb. You're gonna love it.
I'm sure. But not now.
Okay. Fine. Since you don't have time to help me out now, I won't help you out later.

What's that suppose to mean?
When you become defense attorneys I'll take all my business elsewhere.

You've just managed to alleviate all my future worries of being over-worked and under-paid. Thanks brother.
We should get this in writing.

This new book, The Art of How To Get a Woman To Say Yes, is all I need to get a date with Shonda.
I'll believe it when I see it, Sal.
Shonda, your name is Shonda, right?
Yes
And you have a brother name Hector?
Yes
And another brother name Armando?
Yes
Will you go out with me?
Yes--I just did.   When I agreed to meet you here.
Another book? The Art of Asking The Right Questions. Didn't go so good with Shonda, huh lover boy?
Shut up, clown. I'm readin.

So, you go to law school with Shonda. How'd you get in?
I went to college for four years and earned a bachelor degree. Then I got accepted.

You did all that? I bought me one of them bachelor degree's at MacArthur Park for a hundred bucks!
That much, huh.

I guess college don't make you so smart after all!

Some politicians consistently vilify Latinos. I wonder what they'd like to see?
STOP! Hands on top of your head! Drop to your knees!
POLICE
Are you an American citizen?
yes
can you prove it?
I have my ID in my wallet
Thats not good enough! Can you recite the star spangled banner?
What? you `ve got to be kidding You have to be kidding !!
That's not how it goes! You are under arrest!
I'd hate to think about it.

So I say to you kids, playing basketball everyday won't make you a winner.

But studying your lessons and doing your homework daily will make you a winner in the classroom and in life.

Mr. Hakeem, how much money do you make compared to Lebron James?

Don't be so hard on yourself, Hakeem. Anybody would've gotten laughed out of the classroom with that answer

You got
a license?
Suspended.
You?
Revoked

Is it
registered?
Yeah...
to somebody

Is it yours?
Possession is nine
tenths of the law,
right?

We checked off all the
hood requirements.
Let's cruise!

What are you smiling about, Sal?
I was thinking about my first date with Shonda.
I got fifty bucks says that never happened.
Cool. First, me and Shonda had a nice dinner, followed by a movie.
Back at her place we were alone so we cuddled on the sofa.
I still don't believe it.. Then what happened?
Well, I woke up.
You never said it was a dream.
I never said it wasn't. You owe me fifty!

You're gonna like this movie, Hector.
What's it about?

It's called The Crush.
A guy don't return a girl's love
so she makes his life
a living hell.

I don't think so.
Do you have another
movie?
This is my house!
We're watching
The Crush!

This feels creepy.
I'm going home.
Fine! Remember,
I-know-where-
you-live!

Where are you two going?

Our clique is gonna rumble with the other neighborhood clique over our turf!
yeah!

Why do you want to fight other guys over property neither of you own?
burrp!

Because the store on that corner has the cheapest beer in town !
YEAH!

Look at your brother, Armando. Flowers and candy just cause it's Valentines Day. What a simp!
Yeah. Real men don't go out like that.

Hello pretty senorita. Why be alone when you could get lucky with a Latin lover.
Get lost, creep!

When my first rap CD comes out I'm gonna make a grip of money.
For sure, Hector.
The first car I'm gonna buy will be a Jaguar.
Cool. We'll pick up girls late night on Sunset.
Every jam on my CD is gonna be a hit too.
I'll be the first to'pick up a bootleg copy, homie!
I only make money if you buy it in a store.
They sell CD's in stores?

I've been thinking about playing a sport.
Sammy, as long as I've known you, you've never played any sport.
That's why it's about time I start. It's a good way to keep the body in shape.
So are you gonna give up beer and cigarettes too?
Maybe.
What's the catch, Sammy. There's something you're not telling me
Did you see all those mistresses Tiger Woods had?
I should have guessed.

What's wrong, Hector?
A judge threw my discrimination lawsuit against the LAPD out of court today
Why did you file a lawsuit?
The LAPD wouldn't let me and some of my friends go on a ride-along the way they do for other citizens
So why did the judge throw your lawsuit out?
The police showed up with evidence that some of my friends had already been on a ride-along... while they were under arrest!

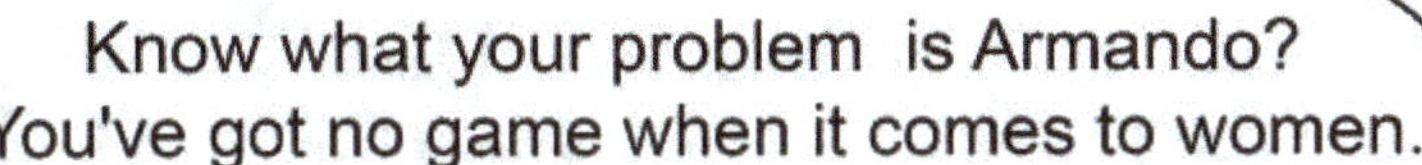

Know what your problem is Armando? You've got no game when it comes to women.
And you do? I suppose you club them over the head and drag them back to your cave.

That stuff is outdated. With modern women you've got to use a modern approach.
Such as?
When I step to a woman, I lie, keep lying, and never get caught in a lie!

You sound like a modern day moron.
But my technique works.
And what happens if you do get caught in a lie?

That's easy. I just lie my way out of it.

Hector, you're a great rapper and I'm your number one fan.
True that.
One day you'll be rich and famous and I'll still be there in your corner.
Yeah, we cool like that.
And maybe when that day comes we can like, think about matrimony.
What!? I mean--no comprende, amigo!
You don't understand? Want me to repeat it in Spanish?
You said matrimony. I don't speak that word in any language!

Where are you coming from, Sammy?
I had a dinner date with Shonda Ortega.

Did not!
Did too! Go read some more of your 'how to get a girl' books, loser boy.

I just got off the phone with Shonda. Her 'mother'invited you to dinner with the family

Did I forget to mention the other Ortega's were there too? That's because the candle light illuminated me and Shonda, while temporarily blocking the others out of our existence.
You should shut up before I temporarily 'knock' you out of my existence.

People like to say that I'm militant. Personally, I find that term offensive.
Passionate is a better word to describe me. Proud of my heritage and passionate about fighting for the rights of Latino people.
Hello General Ortega. It's an honor to serve with you, Ma'am.
Perhaps I could soften my approach a little.

Shonda won't go out with me because she thinks I'm not focused on a career.
I know. Same here.

She doesn't know about all my work as a TV person. I was on that show 'Cops' three times!
That's right.

And what about you? You were on that show, 'America's Stupid Criminals.'
True that... true that...

I'm not feeling the idea of sharing that with the world, though
Yeah...good point!

Linda, every time we're together we argue, and half the time I don't even know why

What do you mean you don't know why? We argue because you don't understand women.

We argue because men are selfish and usually out for themselves. We argue because men are not considerate, compassionate, or sensitive to a woman's needs.
Do you need any more reasons why we argue, Armando?
No. I'm good.

I was going to say we argue because she has a bad temper.
But a man's gotta know when to hold up and when to fold up

Shonda, if you're still not seeing anyone, do I still have a chance?
Sure Sal. You've got the same chance as before.
Didn't you tell him before he had no chance?
He'll figure it out.
BUS STOP
I still got a chance !
I got the same chance !
I ...
bus stop
Aw man, that's cold!

Can you describe the man that robbed you?
He was about fifty-and Hispanic. He had a bald head-and Hispanic. He weighed about three hundred pounds -and Hispanic.

You're only arresting me cause I'm Hispanic!
No, we wouldn't do that. You fit the description.

I demand that you let my brother go! You only arrested him because he's Hispanic!
No, you're wrong. You're brother happens to fit the description.

Hey Sarge, should I go upstairs and arrest Lieutenant Lopez? She sorta fit the description too!

I see bright lights in your future,Hector
I knew it!

I see stretch limousine's and millions of fans.
I was born for this!

And there's a beautiful woman.
Shakira?
She's more local
You--I suppose.

Yes! Hector, you must be psychic too!
It don't take ESP to see where you were heading with this

Why is it when a Latino immigrant commits an infraction of the law, no matter how minor, it gets blown up by the media?
I beg to differ, Miss Ortega. Here at WKWK-L we strive to be fair and impartial.
I have my doubts, Mr. station president. And I'll be watching with a keen eye for bias reporting.
I'm sure you will Ms.
OMG Mr. station president, two Latino immigrants were just issued citations for jaywalking!
Did you call the Senator?
He's on hold for you.
What would you like me to do, Senator?
RUN THE STORY! RUN THE STORY!

Shakira, my bonita senorita. I love it when you say, Ay Papi! Loca! Loca! Loca!
Hector, wake up. You're talking in your sleep.

Huh? Oh. What did I say?
Nothing to worry about.

I didn't say anything ...embarrassing?
No. Well, I gotta go.
Alright.

The world deserves to see this!

Some sky.
Yes
Some moon
Uh huh.
Some stars
Really nice.
Some night.
BLAM
'Some' can remember their girlfriend's birthday!

I'll bet Shonda couldn't wait to go riding with me if I pull up in a top of the line Jaguar. I saw George Lopez driving one on TV, and I've got his address!
Naw, I'll bet she'd prefer a top of the line Hummer. Shaq Diesel got one and I know where he lives!
That Jag will make it back here faster than that Hummer.
I'll be cruising the hills, homie. Cruising the hills.
BUS STOP

Armando, do you think I'm militant?
Somewhat.
Somewhat? What's that suppose to mean?

I've already had an argument with Linda today, Shonda. I'm not looking for another one.
I'm not gonna argue, Armando. I just want your honest opinion.

Well, at times you do come off as militant- by definition of the word, that is.
I SUPPOSE ANY WOMAN NOT AFRAID TO EXPRESS HER OPINION IS MILITANT BY DEFINITION OF THE WORD IN YOUR WORLD, RIGHT ARMANDO?!!

YES DRILL SERGEANT!!
Really Armando?
Sorry, impulsive reaction

Hector, why do you keep those dark sunglasses on, even at night?
I don't want my groupies to bum rush me when I step outside the door.

News flash, Hector. You don't have any groupies.
Oh they're out there. They just don't recognize me with my shades on.

Hector, you have no groupies and no record deal. You've never even preformed in front of an audience!

Don't hate, Mando--participate! Maybe one day I'll give you a job carrying an umbrella to keep too much sun from beaming on top of my head.
It's too late for that, bro.

I sent my rap demo to a major record label.
What'd they say?
I told them that my style was unique.
Sounds good.
And I told them rapping has been my dream since junior high.
Cool. So when is your CD coming out?
The executive said, 'over my dead body', so...
That sounds sarcastic. Want me to call the homies?
I want to live big time, Sammy. Not 'do' big time.

I hate this newspaper. Every time I write a letter expressing my views they won't print it
They won't print a well written letter that goes against the grain of society. But if an idiot writes a letter they'll print it so fast he won't know what hit him
I wrote a letter to the paper. I told them the police don't like me cause I'm a vato loco rapper
Look, they printed it!
POW
Da did one a y'all ha hit me?
That's amazing
Told you

The person who most inspired me to become an Attorney is Johnny Cochran. He won millions of dollars for people of color that were victims of police brutality.

Yeah, but he had to play the race card to win the OJ trial

Another crack like that and I'm gonna remember when I use to be a big bad brother coming straight outta Compton!

Did I say 'race card?' I meant 'ace card.' That's it. He played an ace.

Linda, I'm gonna stay away from Hector for awhile. Once he realizes he misses me he'll come running.

Good luck, Lucy.

Hector, what a surprise! I knew you'd miss me, baby
You're standing on my doorstep.

But you must have known I'd be here. Why else would you come?

Today is my anniversary, Linda. It's been exactly one month since me and Hector have been dating.

You mean it's been one month since you've been chasing him.
Whatever. Anyway, I'm trying to come up with something nice to do for him.

My grandmother use to say the way to a man's heart is through his stomach.
Food is a good idea. Maybe a bottle of champagne and some caviar to celebrate.

We're talking about Hector, Lucy. A bottle of beer and a bucket of chicken is all it takes to satisfy.

Sal, you want to know the secret to impressing my sister? She likes cake--chocolate cake.

Sammy, Shonda like ice cream. Strawberry ice cream.

I don't understand why Sammy and Sal bought me cake and ice cream. It's not my birthday.
I might have kinda mislead them a little. Mmmm, I love chocolate cake and strawberry ice cream.
ICE CR

Hey, why'd you do that? You got cake and ice cream out the deal.
So did you!
ICE CR

Sal, I'm curious. Why'd you spend a hundred bucks for a bachelor degree at MacArthur Park?

I want to show Shonda that we're on the same education level.
I see. But Sal, don't you think there might be a difference?

Duh--yeah. She got her's the hard way and I got mine the easy way. When she finish law school I'm gonna buy me one of them law degrees too.
Course,they a little more expensive.

Plan on blowing her mind, huh?
You better believe it, Pancho.

Mr. Hakeem, I thought about what you said, and I think I get it.
Get what, Derrick

There's more to life than admiring Lebron James because he's a great basketball player.
That's right.
There are more important things than winning lots of games, making tons of money, and going to conference championships.
I'm proud of you, Derrick. Now you're on the right track.

I like the younger players cause they be throwing money in the clubs and making it rain!

This is just a test. I can do this...I can do this...

Know what our problem is Sal, we're spending to much time chasing Shonda.
You're right.
Let's make a pack, no more Shonda Ortega.
Yeah, let's get back to the players we use to be.
Hello Sammy--hold on, I got another call.
Hello Sal, let me put you on three way with Sammy.
Uh, I was just calling her to say goodby
Yeah...me too.

CRUISING DOWN THE STREET IN MY 6-4 SIGNED A RECORD DEAL AND IM READY TO BLOW. GOT THE CASH AND THE GIRLS AND THE CRIB AND THE FAME
You dont even have a job so that still make you lame!
What, did I show up in your dream again?
Not phisically but I know your voice!!

STORE

The pizzas were right here then they were gone!

I just turned my back for a second and the drinks vanished!

Hello my favorite Ortega family! I got pizzas for everybody!
And I got drinks!

Shonda, don't ask! Sammy, Sal, don't tell! Let's just thank The Almighty and enjoy our meal!

OTHER BOOKS
BY
CALEB CARTER.

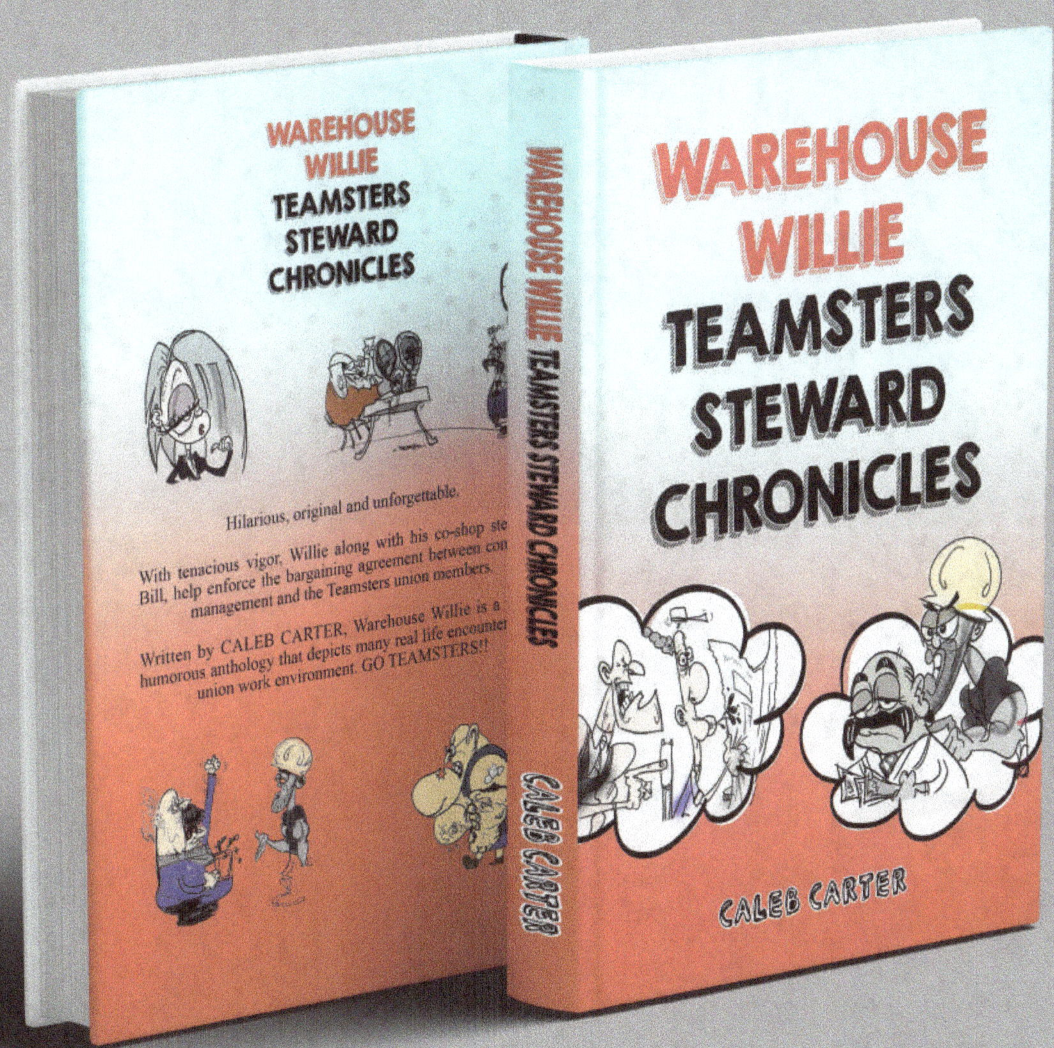

WAREHOUSE WILLIE
TEAMSTERS STEWARD CHRONICLES
Hilarious, original and unforgettable.
With tenacious vigor, Willie along with his co-shop steward Bill, help enforce the bargaining agreement between company management and the Teamsters union members.
Written by CALEB CARTER, Warehouse Willie is a humorous anthology that depicts many real life encounters in a union work environment. GO TEAMSTERS!!
WAREHOUSE WILLIE TEAMSTERS STEWARD CHRONICLES CALEB CARTER
WAREHOUSE WILLIE
TEAMSTERS STEWARD CHRONICLES
CALEB CARTER